Below is a list of the original Doctor Dolittle books written by Hugh Lofting and published by J. B. Lippincott Company of Philadelphia and New York:

BOOK CLUB EDITION

Doctor Dolittle
and the
Pirates

Hugh Lofting's
Doctor Dolittle
and the
Pirates

by Al Perkins/Illustrated by Philip Wende

ADAPTED FOR BEGINNING READERS

BEGINNER BOOKS   A Division of Random House, Inc.

J K L   8 9

Doctor Dolittle and his animals
were sailing home from Africa.
The pushmi-pullyu was on watch.
"I see no danger in front of us,"
he said with his front head.

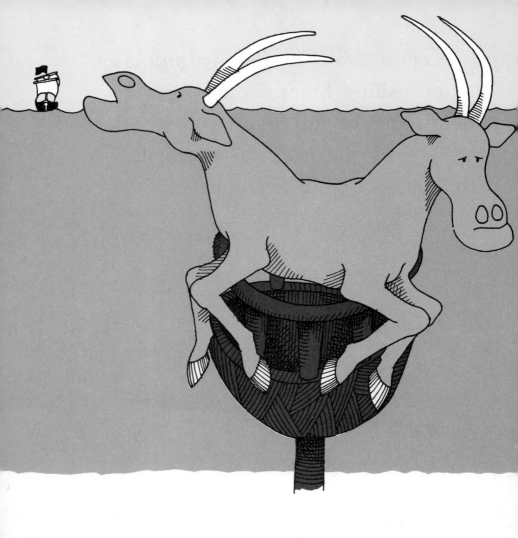

"But I do see danger in back of us,"
the pushmi-pullyu said with his
back head.

Doctor Dolittle looked through
his spyglass. "It's a pirate ship,"
he said. "We must get away from it!"

The pirate ship came closer and
closer. The pirates waved swords
and knives and pistols.

The pushmi-pullyu jumped
down from the mast.
"How can we get away?"
he asked with both
his heads.

"Take a deep breath, all of you,"
Doctor Dolittle said.
"Then blow into our sails."
They all blew.
The pushmi-pullyu blew the hardest
of all. He blew into the sails
with both his mouths.
The boat began to go much faster.
They left the pirate ship behind.

Now Doctor Dolittle and his animals
came to some islands.
Singing birds flew out to meet them.

"Ah," said Doctor Dolittle.
"These must be the Canary Islands.
I can hear the canaries singing."
They sailed into the beautiful bay.

11

Just then a small black rat
ran across the deck.
"Ahem! Pardon me, Doctor Dolittle,"
said the rat. "But I must tell you
something. This is a bad ship.
She's not safe. She's going to sink."
"How do you know?" asked the Doctor.

"We rats always know," the rat said.
"The tips of our tails get that
tingly feeling, like when your foot's
asleep. Right now our tails all tell
us that, before tonight, this boat
will sink to the bottom of the sea!"

"Come, brother rats," the rat shouted.
"Don't stay in this boat, or you'll
all be drowned! Follow me!"
Rats came running from everywhere.
They jumped off the boat and ran away.
"Thank you very much for warning us,"
Doctor Dolittle shouted.
"I'll remember what you said."

Then Doctor Dolittle and his animals
went ashore.
The canaries showed them the way.

They all were hot and tired
and thirsty. They carried pails
to fill up with fresh water.

The canaries led them to a beautiful
pool of cool, clear water. Here
they swam and splashed and played.

Doctor Dolittle took a bath.
The pushmi-pullyu drank and drank.
Dab-Dab quacked with joy.

Then the canaries took them to a
lovely hillside and sang to them.
But all of a sudden, Too-Too flew
up from the beach.
"Doctor!" he cried. "Wake up!"

"Is our boat sinking?" asked
the Doctor sleepily. "The rat said
it would sink before tonight."
"No," said Too-Too. "It's not
sinking. But the pirates have just
sailed into the bay! Come and look!"

They all raced to the edge of the
cliff. They looked down at the beach.
And they saw the black pirate ship!
It was in the bay. And it was
right next to Doctor Dolittle's boat.
"We must go down there," said the
Doctor. "We must see what those
pirates are doing."

They hurried down the rough,
narrow path.
They went as fast as they dared.

The pushmi-pullyu got to the beach
first. He looked out from behind
a big rock. "The pirates are all
on our boat!" he said. "They are
looking for things to steal."

"Let them have our old boat,"
said Doctor Dolittle.
"I have an idea."

"We'll take their big ship and
sail away!" said the Doctor.
"But don't make a noise.
Don't let them hear us."

Jip pulled up the anchor—very
quietly. Dab-Dab and Gub-Gub
set the sails—very quietly.
Doctor Dolittle took the wheel.

Then something
terrible happened. . . .

THE PUSHMI-PULLYU SNEEZED!

The pirates heard that sneeze!
They rushed to the rail to see
what was going on.
Ben Ali, the pirate leader, saw
Doctor Dolittle at the wheel of
his big black ship.
"They're stealing our ship!"
he shouted. "Stop them, mates!"

The pirates grabbed long ropes.
They swung from the little boat
to the big black ship.
They waved their knives and
guns and swords.

Ben Ali yelled, "You were going
to run away in my big ship, were you?
Now you listen to me! Give me
your money, or I'll throw you
into the sea."

Then Ben Ali saw Dab-Dab and
Gub-Gub. "What's this?"
he shouted. "A nice plump duck
and a nice fat pig! Get them,
mates! We'll have pork chops
and roast duck for dinner."

Gub-Gub and Dab-Dab shook with
fright. "Please!" they begged
the Doctor. "Don't let them eat us!"

Just then Too-Too whispered,
"Make the pirates go back to our boat.
It might sink very soon.
Then it will take all these bad men
to the bottom of the sea."
"A fine idea!" the Doctor whispered
back. "I'll try it."

"See here, Ben Ali!" Doctor Dolittle
said. "You want our money.
Take it! It's on our little boat.
There's a trunk full of gold there."

Ben Ali shouted to the pirates,
"Back to the other boat, mates!
There's gold on that old boat."

The pirates cheered and shouted.
They slid down the masts.
They swung back to the little boat.

The pirates raced all over
Doctor Dolittle's old boat.
They searched everywhere,
looking for the gold.

Then suddenly something happened.
Ben Ali looked down at the deck.
It was leaking.
Water was shooting up into the air!

The leaks got bigger and bigger.
The water rose higher and higher.
The old boat began to sink.

The Doctor and his animals watched.
"Hooray!" Jip barked. "She's sinking,
just like the rat said she would."

Ben Ali and the pirates jumped
into the water.
The old boat plunged deep down
into the sea. It made a terrible
gurgling sound as it went.

But the pirates were all good
swimmers. They still had their
knives and swords and pistols.
They swam toward Doctor Dolittle
and his animals. "We'll get you yet!"
Ben Ali shouted as he swam.

Then the pirates yelled with fright.
Something was chasing them.
"Look out!" one pirate shouted.
"It's a big shark!"

"It's a lot of sharks!"
yelled Ben Ali.
"Help!
The sharks are chasing us!"

One big shark poked his nose out
of the water. "Doctor Dolittle,"
he said, "you are a good man.
You are kind to all animals, even
sharks. So we are your friends.
But these pirates are bad men.
We will be happy to eat them for you,
one by one. Then they won't
trouble you any more."

"Please," begged Ben Ali,
"don't let the sharks get us!
We'll do anything you say!"

"Very well," said Doctor Dolittle.
"You cannot be pirates any more.
You must live on shore.
You must grow birdseed
for the canaries."

"Birdseed!"
The pirates groaned.
"What a job for pirates!"

But the pirates had no choice.
They swam to the shore
and climbed out of the water.

Then Doctor Dolittle and his friends
sailed off in the big black pirate
ship. The canaries flew above
and sang good-bye. The sharks
led the way out of the bay.

Doctor Dolittle and his pets
went down into the cabin.
"It's beautiful!" cried Too-Too.
There were thick, soft carpets.

There were beds with silk sheets.
There were treasure chests
full of money and jewels.
And there were good things to eat!

After supper, the Doctor and his pets
went up on deck. The pushmi-pullyu
was on top of the mast.
"I see no danger ahead of us,"
he said with his front head.
"And I see no danger behind us,"
he said with his back head.
"Then," said Doctor Dolittle, "we
shall all get safely home to England."

And that's exactly what they did.

61